First published by Parragon in 2012

Parragon
Queen Street House
4 Queen Street
Bath BA1 1HE, UK
www.parragon.com

ISBN 978-1-4454-6737-5

Printed in China

Count to 10 with a mouse

Bath • New York • Singapore • Hong Kong • Cologne • Delhi
Melbourne • Amsterdam • Johannesburg • Auckland • Shenzhen

There was a little mouse

no **bigger**
than a
mole,

who lived in a round place

that he called a **hole.**

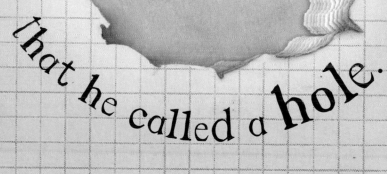

He tried
to Count
his

nose

he tried
to count
his
toes.

He said,
"I'd better
learn to
count,"
and so the
story goes.

1 mouse

One mouse, took one

look, at **one** book,

that had **one** hole
to run through.

2 holes

Then the mouse ran through the book,

the mouse ran through the book.

He ran onto the next page,

to
take a
little
look.

3 fish

And there, what does he see?
And there, what does he see?

Three little fishes

Swimming in the sea.

Then the mouse ran through the book,
the mouse ran through the book.
He ran onto the next page
to take a little look.

4 monkeys

And here, what does he see?
And here, what does he see?

Four little monkeys

Swinging in a tree.

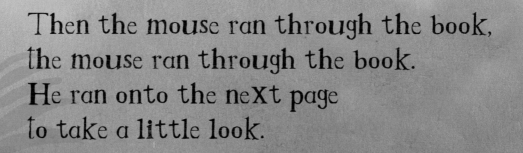

Then the mouse ran through the book,
the mouse ran through the book.
He ran onto the next page
to take a little look.

5 butterflies

And here, great sakes alive!
And here, great sakes alive!

Here he found five butterflies,

one, two, three, four, five.

Then the mouse ran through the book,
the mouse ran through the book.
He ran onto the next page
to take a little look.

6 pussycats

And in amongst the mix.
And in amongst the mix.

Six little pussycats
are all in a fix.

So the mouse ran through the book,
the mouse ran through the book.
He ran onto the next page
to take a little look.

7 apples

And there, what does he see?
And there, what does he see?

seven little apples

upon an apple tree.

Then the mouse ran through the book,
the mouse ran through the book.
He ran onto the next page
to take a little look.

8 crows

And here is what he saw.
And here is what he saw.

caw!

Eight shiny black crows

caw!

caw!

learning how to caw.

caw!

W!

Then the mouse ran through the book,
the mouse ran through the book.
He ran into the next page
to take a little look.

9 o'clock

Here everything is fine
The clock has just struck nine.
Nine o'clock is nine o'clock
and everything is fine.

o Hickory Dickory Dock,

the mouse ran **up** the clock.

Then Dockery Hickory Dock
the mouse ran down the clock.

Then the mouse ran through the book,
the mouse ran through the book.
He ran onto the next page
to take a little look.

1   2   3   4   5

And when he got to ten.

And when he got to ten.

He turned around the other way

and ran right back again.

The
End